# MALINVESTMENT

## MICHAEL KINGSWOOD

# CONTENTS


*About This Book*      v

Malinvestment      1

*Message From The Author*      37
*Mailing List*      39
*Supporting Patronage*      41
*About The Author*      43
*More Books By Michael Kingswood*      45

# ABOUT THIS BOOK

It sucks being the god of malinvestment, the force behind economic downturns.

Tom has been trying to use his position to shape the world for the better for as long as he can remember. Trying, and failing. Every time.

But what if he'd been going about it the wrong way all this time?

Enjoy the book! After you're done, please come to Michael's website and sign up for his mailing list at michaelkingswood.com/newsletter-signup/.  Guaranteed to be spam free, he uses it to announce new releases and special promotions for his fans.

# MALINVESTMENT

My boss is staring at me from across his desk. His eyes are squinty, drawing his eyebrows down until it looks like he has a black unibrow over his face, and his lips are drawn thinly into a displeased scowl.

I'm pretty sure I'm about to be fired.

Again.

It's not the first time I've been in this situation, and it probably won't be the last. But it never gets easier. Every time the failure weighs on my shoulders until I feel I cannot move, and I find myself envying Atlas, that poor bastard.

Gods aren't supposed to feel rejection—to feel useless—like this. At least Atlas can take on his burden with a sense of pride.

I don't even get that.

Pete. That's my boss' name. Even if I had been able to forget, it was always plain to see on the faded white nametag he wears on his right breast every day, pinned to the white collared shirt that makes up the upper part of his work uniform. Pete clears his throat, and his eyes drop to the surface of his desk, where his morning coffee—procured from the store's industrial-sized percolator but, I'd noticed, never paid for —is leaving a spreading stain on his desk blotter.

"Look Tom," he says, "I'm a devout man. But I told you when you came to work here. I can't have any of this god-stuff going on in the store." He tries to manage a comforting smile as his eyes lift back up to meet mine, and fails. Instead, he tries a pitiful approximation of commiseration. "We're operating on a shoestring margin here, and..." He trails off, and his expression practically pleads for me to pick up the slack.

What else can I do? I oblige him.

"I understand, and you've been more than patient." I add as he opens his mouth to interject, sudden nervousness showing on his face, "And fair."

He closes his mouth, looking at me with an expression that combines disbelief and gratitude.

"Well," he says as he draws himself up, trying to look more confident than he feels, "I'll be honest. I never understood why you took this job to begin with. I mean, you're..." He trails off and makes a vague movement with his left hand, a gesture that says I surely know what he's trying to say. "You've got resources, and...well, you know."

Ordinarily, I'd let it go with that. Because I know exactly what he means, and for most of us, he would be right. But I'm not most of us, and right now I suddenly can find no reason to help Pete assuage his own guilt by pretending he is correct.

It's a failing of mine, letting my emotions take control when doing so would not be advantageous. But at this moment, the frustration and, frankly, humiliation of having to endure this...again...wells up in a rush that I cannot hold back.

I half-chuckle, half-snort, and Pete recoils in his seat.

"Pete," I say, leaning forward and fixing him with a stare that I try very hard to keep unblinking. "I'm the god of malinvestment. Do you know what malinvestment is?"

Pete shakes his head, unable to look away from my gaze.

"That's when businesses misinterpret the data in the marketplace and make investments in areas that end up being less than optimal, or even wasteful. When enough businesses do it at once, the economy as a whole goes from boom," I raise my left hand toward the ceiling, "to bust." I drop the hand into my lap. Pete blinks, and I manage a wry grin. "It's not exactly a lucrative gig, and I have to pay rent like everyone else."

Pete's face goes pale. "You..." He stops, clears his throat. "You're saying you cause recessions?" His voice comes out in a near croak, and his eyes have gone wide.

I wave off his words with my right hand. "No, of course not. That's done by millions of people and thousands of businesses doing what they do. Even a god can't control that. Believe me, I've tried." I sigh, dropping my own eyes now. "Do you know how it is to know it's coming, to feel the inevitability of it, to know about all the people who are going to lose their jobs, to feel yourself growing stronger as the energy of it flows through you, like you're its lightning rod, and to know there's nothing you can do to stop it?"

A long silence, and then Pete clears his throat. "Well. Your final check will be ready in two weeks."

Another pause, and he won't meet my eyes this time. "Sorry, Tom."

He is *way* past uncomfortable now. I think I can see a tremble in his torso, and that little vein on the side of his temple is throbbing quickly.

I stand up and shake his hand, which is clammy and limp as always.

"Been nice working with you," I say before I turn to leave his office, and then his little coffee shop, for the last time.

It's not an entirely true statement, but not exactly a lie, either.

Working here sure beat the alternative.

---

It's RAINING as I step out of the coffee shop, a light splattering just greater than a drizzle but not quite enough to really be respectable. I take a minute and flip up the collar of my trench coat, then, hunching my shoulders and lowering my gaze from the falling droplets, I hurry out of the doorway and onto the sidewalk.

I turn left, pausing only long enough to let a young woman who's talking on her cell phone, oblivious to everyone and everything around her, pass ahead of me.

Part of me thinks it would have served her right to run into her, to knock her sprawling.

I push that part down viciously. It's not her fault I just got fired, not her I'm angry with.

And I *am* angry. Now that I've left Pete's domain, it comes forth from that place of power within me, and I feel it course through my veins, urging me to lash out at something.

How *dare* he!

I find I'm clenching my fists as I stalk down the sidewalk toward the bus stop at the end of the block, and force myself to relax.

Deep breath.

Better.

I reach the bus stop and stop at the outskirts of the small crowd of half a dozen people who are waiting there. They're all sodden, like I'm becoming, and dressed in clothing that ranges from halfway decent to thrift store reject. One and all, they look glum, joyless.

But that could just be the rain getting to them.

"It's coming soon."

The voice at my left elbow draws my gaze, and the anger returns again. I recognize the young man from inside Pete's shop: lightly tanned with curly black hair and dark brown eyes, a smirking grin, and the sort of stylishly casual attire that screams it costs a bundle. He's the reason I don't have a job anymore.

The kid leans in toward me, his eyes bright. "It is, isn't it?"

I scowl at him. Say nothing.

He glances about and shuffles a bit closer, his voice lowering. "Where's it going to start?"

I roll my eyes. "Kid, I told you before. Check my website. My office hours are -"

"6 til 10:30 pm on Tuesdays and Thursdays, I know. This can't wait, though." He shakes his head and tries to grin conspiratorially. It just makes him look stupid. "I think we can help each other."

I can't help it. I laugh. Bitterly, scornfully, up-roariously.

I've seen this a thousand times. Some schmuck

who thinks he can use me to make a buck when it all hits the fan.

Pinching the wetness from my eyes with my thumb and forefinger, I shake my head. "I've heard this one before, kid. What, you want a short-sale tip or something?" I shake my head. "Doesn't work that way. And even if it did, I wouldn't give it to you."

He blinks, recoils a half-step, suddenly looking unsure of himself. "That's not what I -"

"No? Well, that would certainly be a refreshing change of pace."

A large white bus, covered in advertisements for the metropolitan art gallery, along with other smaller ads for an assortment of bars and restaurants, comes to a stop with a soft squeal of breaks. A moment later, its door swings open, and two passengers get off. The others in the queue begin boarding, and I move to follow.

"Divine One, I -"

That was going way too far. I fix him with a contemptuous gaze that stops him cold. "Don't call me that."

He opens his mouth to start again, and I cut him off.

"Don't call me anything at all. You cost me my job today. Piss off."

When the bus pulls away, he's still standing there, looking stunned.

Looking stupid.

---

THING IS, the kid's right.

I've felt it coming for months now. It started small, as it always does, a tingling on the back on my neck as I walked into the mall. A surge that didn't quite resemble adrenalin as I watched the business news on CNBC. Little feelings and signs, here and there, getting slowly stronger as the weeks went by.

And with them, I am becoming stronger as well.

Back in my apartment, a crappy studio on the third floor of a crappier building on the south side of town, I take a minute to look at myself in the mirror beside my front door as I hang up my thoroughly soaked trench coat.

I look younger than I did just six months ago. The crows feet at the corners of my eyes are lighter, my frown lines more like valleys than canyons. I stand straighter, tire less easily. Don't need to sleep as much. A couple weekends ago, with a nameless girl I almost literally stumbled into at a bar, I learned I can go all night again, like I used to back in the good old days.

The days before I got this god gig.

With a sigh, I turn away from the mirror and cross my cramped little room to a small bookshelf that stands beside my single window. The shelf is only about four feet tall. Atop it lives a bottle of Glenfiddich and a pair of glasses. I pour myself a couple fingers and replace the bottle, then collapse into my little stuffed chair and take a sip.

I try to avoid it, but I also begin to think.

Yeah, the kid is right. The boom is getting ready to bust. Probably sometime in the next six months to a year.

And, like always, I'm powerless to do anything about it except watch myself return to youth as I absorb its destructive energy, feed on it.

This is not how it is supposed to be, being a god.

I WAKE to a knocking on my door. Not particularly loud knocking, but insistent.

I groan from where I sit in my chair, the empty glass that used to hold my scotch—two glasses of it —still resting in my left hand on the chair's arm, and will whoever it is to just go away. Leave me alone.

The knock comes again.

I mutter under my breath and force myself upright, then run my right hand through my hair, pushing it back from my eyes as I scan the wall for my clock. 7:15 pm.

It's not yet dark outside my window, but it feels like midnight.

"Just a minute," I bellow as I stumble to the sink in my little kitchenette and pour some water into the glass. I chug it and clunk the glass down onto the counter, then trudge over to the door and pull it open.

The kid's standing there, a mixture of nervousness and determination on his lean face.

I roll my eyes. "Jesus Christ," I say, and the irony of my own words is not lost on me. I take a breath. "What the hell do *you* want?"

The kid swallows. "Divi -" My quickly deepening scowl makes him stop mid-word. For a second, he almost looks like he's going to leave, and I feel relief. Then he lets me have it. "It's Tuesday," he says, simply.

I blink at him, uncomprehending.

His eyebrows rise. "Your office hours?"

I have to work hard to suppress a groan. But he's right, isn't he? It *is* Tuesday, and these *are* my advertised office hours. Much as I want to, I can't just turn him away, not now, at this hour. That simply is not how things are done in the pantheon. And while there would not be consequences, per say, I would have to hear about it for years, if not decades, every time we have a meeting.

I really don't need that sort of annoyance.

So, I roll my eyes and turn away from the door. As I walk into the room, I veer toward the kitchenette and grab up my glass, then put another couple fingers into it from my nearly depleted bottle before collapsing into my chair again.

By then, the kid has closed the door behind himself and is standing at the foot of my bed, watching me with uncertain eyes.

I take a swig, waving with my hand for him to get on with it.

He glances around my room, and I can tell from the expression on his face it is not what he expected from a god. But then, he probably thinks gods are all like those Greek assholes are reputed to be: always drinking the best wine, turning into showers of gold, and seducing virgins. If he'd ever met them, he would know better.

"Ah," he says, finally. "What...do I call you, if not..." He trails off.

"Tom," I say, taking another sip. "Name's Tom."

The kid blinks as though surprised, and I'm tempted to say something snarky. But what the hell. He's here, might as well let him speak.

"Ok...Tom." He reaches into the pocket of his cargo pants and pulls out a small spiral notebook. "I've been doing some research. Now, correct me if I'm wrong."

He probably is.

He flips the book open. "You weren't always a god. At some point it was turned over to you, right?"

I figure I might as well get good and loopy, so I take another sip. Only way I figure this is going to be tolerable.

The kid takes my silence for assent and nods his head. "Right. So what happened to the old guy?"

I stop, my glass half-lowered from my lips. "What do you mean?"

He cocks his head to the side, looks at me weirdly. "After he turned over the mantle to you, did he give you any instruction, or...?" He waves his free hand.

I snort and finish lowering my glass. "Don't work that way, kid. Old god retires, he goes to his rest. New god comes into the fold. Just my dumb luck I happened to be the most un-lucky son of a bitch around when old Tisdale had enough of it."

"When was that?"

I shrug. "Crash of '29. I was about to jump out a window on Wall Street, when all of a sudden..." I leave over; no need to tell that story again, and really I don't want to think about it.

"So he didn't talk to you, or anything?"

"Kid, I didn't even know what happened until a week later. One minute, I'm on the ledge about to step off, the next some guy steps out onto the ledge with me. He touches me on the shoulder with this sad little smile and jumps, and suddenly I feel like the world is my oyster and I can do no wrong. I was stronger than I ever had been, more energetic." I frown. "Thought of jumping just went away completely." After a second, I add, "Too bad," then sip some more scotch.

The kid nods again, and his face lights up with

something like excitement. And maybe...satisfaction? "So this Tisdale bought it, and you became the god. But you never had anyone to teach you how to do your job." He grins, almost in triumph.

Oh for the love of...

I roll my head back and stare up at the ceiling. I can't help but laugh. When I finally lower my gaze a minute later, the kid doesn't look quite so smug.

"You think I didn't try that, kid?" I say to his stupid face. "I'm not an idiot. I sought out von Mises. Keynes. Hayek. Friedman. Freaking Krugman! You name an economist with a Nobel or a school named after him, I talked to him. They *all* wanted to talk to me, of course." I can't keep the bitter irony out of my voice; some of those jokers didn't seem to care that I even existed. I raise my left index finger toward the ceiling. "Know what came of all that study?"

The kid shakes his head.

"Jack squat, that's what. I can tell you all about macro and microeconomic theories. All of them. But that doesn't change a damn thing." I blow out a sigh. "I age, get tired. Economy starts slowing down and reversing, I get younger and stronger. I ride the wave of the times, feed on the energy of other people's misfortune." I spit out the words with all the self-loathing I can muster, and that's quite a bit after all these years. "And not a damn thing I can do to change anything or help anyone."

I drop my free hand and finish off my glass. My head is really starting to swim, and I flop back into the cushions of the chair. "I've tried, kid, believe me. Nothing does a lick of good."

He stares at me for a long moment, and I think he's going to take the hint and go away. But then his lips compress into a thin, determined line. "What if I told you I've found a way to change that?"

---

COOPERATION AMONG THE GODS.

It's been done before. Been done a lot, in fact, for obvious reasons. But generally, it only happens when the gods' spheres interrelate somehow, again for obvious reasons.

In between accomplishing nothing with the various academic economists in the world, I pitched trying to work together with Johannes, the god of trade, and after that to the other guys and gals in the economic sphere.

I thought the *academics* gave me the cold shoulder. One and all, my fellow gods of economics said no faster than a good Catholic girl on a first date.

So I gave up on the idea.

I still don't think it'll work, but what can I say? The kid makes a good sales pitch. And, frankly, part of me still has hope that maybe I can find a way to make something good out of my position.

I'd almost forgotten that part of me still existed.

So, in the morning I meet the kid out front of a coffee shop—not Pete's—and thirty minutes later we're standing in front of a well-cared-for brownstone on a street full of them.

The lady who answers the door when the kid knocks is a knock-out. Tall and willowy, olive skin, sharp grey-green eyes, and flowing auburn hair. Her skirt and blouse are casually conservative, but accentuate her curves just enough to draw the eye.

Fortunately, it's not raining today, or the effect would have been spoiled by a raincoat.

"Hello, Charles," she says to the kid when she sees him, then gestures for him to lead the way.

The kid nods to her, more a half-bow, then turns and walks over to where his car is parked. I turn to follow and the lady falls into step beside me.

"You're Tom, of Malinvestment, right?"

I nod.

"Gretchen," she says, and extends her hand to me. "Psychological Disorders."

I almost stumble over a crack in the sidewalk. But I catch myself and manage to not look the complete fool as I shake hands.

Her grip is surprisingly firm and sure of itself.

What in the hell has the kid gotten me into here?

The kid—Charles—gets behind the wheel, and I open the backseat door for Gretchen. I'm a gentleman. Sue me. Once she's settled, I cross to the other side of the car and get in beside her.

Might as well let Charles play chauffeur. Least he can do.

He pulls the car out into traffic and gets going. Stealing a glance at the lovely lady next to me, I speak up. "Time for a little more detail on this scheme of yours, kid."

His eyes flick toward me in the rearview and he tenses for a second. "It'll really be easier just to show you."

Beside me, Gretchen chuckles softly. "Oh, this will be fun."

I can't tell if she's serious or not.

---

FORTY-FIVE MINUTES LATER, we are all sitting around a round wrought iron table in the outdoor seating area of a small cafe. A round waiter who looks as though he would rather be just about anywhere else provides a tea setting, then leaves us to our devices.

Not impressive service, but I do have to compliment the cafe on the tea. I can't place the blend, but it is excellent. It's tempting to just relax and enjoy, but if anything, Charles looks even more tense than he did in the car. So instead, I sip at my cup and throw my grenade.

"Ok, kid. You going to quit screwing around and tell us what your master plan is already?"

Gretchen shoots me a look that's a mix of chagrin—at my tone, for certain—and agreement.

For his part, Charles swallows hard and jerks his head toward the building across the street.

I turn to look in that direction and see a small bookstore directly across the way. It's not a chain, but one of those independent joints that have been cropping up everywhere over the last couple of years. Obviously well-kept, it boasts red and yellow flowers in ceramic pots on either side of the double-door entrance and the usual displays of new releases and future events in the windows. Well, not the usual displays; these are personalized in the way that the ones at Barnes and Noble aren't.

Gives the place a friendly, homey sort of look. I like it immediately. And just as immediately, I note that this did not answer my question in any way at all.

I look back at Charles and raise an eyebrow at him. I can feel the corners of my mouth lowering, as if of their own free will.

He notices as well and blanches, then says hurriedly, "They've been open for twenty-five years.

Were doing well, but just recently started having money problems."

And then it becomes obvious what he has in mind, and I curse under my breath as I set my teacup down—slowly and carefully, of course—on its saucer. "I told you, kid, I can't do anything about that sort of thing. Not how it works. I just -"

He cuts me off, which makes me blink in surprise and shut up, unexpected as it is considering how deferential he's been to this point.

"- Roll with the tide of the times. Yes, I know. You've made that abundantly clear, Tom." His tone is, if not outright disrespectful at least dismissively sarcastic. He gestures toward Gretchen as he continues. "You either can't or won't do anything about it, but she can."

Gretchen has been looking amused as she watched our interaction. Now it is her turn to affect surprise. "I'm sorry. I'm not a businesswoman."

Charles rolls his eyes. "Look." He looks at me more directly. "Correct me if I'm wrong, but economics is basically the study of how people respond to incentives."

His tone expects an answer, so I give him one. "It's a little bit more complicated than that," I say, then shrug and add, "But yeah, pretty much."

Charles nods. "Well that's just psychology." His eyes find Gretchen's. "If he can figure out where they're going wrong..."

She purses her lips. "I can fix it?" She hums tunelessly for a few seconds as she ponders. Then her pursed lips turn into a deep frown. "Your theorem is that poor economic decisions are the result of mental illness?"

It clearly sounds as ludicrous to her as it does to me, but Charles nods.

"Why not? Why would someone choose against their best interests unless -"

My turn to cut him off. "You're assuming the person has perfect information about the choice. That's almost impossible, in reality." I recall many a long discussion with Hayek about that very thing. Took me a while, but I came away convinced he had the right of it.

Charles' shoulders slump and he lowers his gaze toward his teacup. "Well, maybe not mental illness, but something. I mean..." He trails off, and it's clear he's at a loss.

Gretchen's gaze meets mine. She looks troubled, and I can't blame her. I'm about ready to call this meeting over. Then she surprises me.

"How long has your family owned that store, Charles?"

He gives a little jerk and his eyes widen.

Kid shouldn't be surprised when a goddess in the realm of psychology sees right through him.

"My parents are the ones who first opened it," he replied, softly.

Well, that explains things. "That's what you meant yesterday about helping each other." I don't wait for him to nod. I just stand up, pushing my chair back roughly in my haste to leave.

This was a complete waste of time. He doesn't have any grand insight, just pathetic fear for his parents' business. My voice becomes rough as disappointment—a feeling I did not expect to experience in this enterprise—changes to anger within me. "I've heard about enough of this."

I turn to go, but Gretchen's voice stops me.

"We've come all this way. Might as well give it a try, Tom."

I turn my head and look back at her. Try to not let her beauty overpower my sensibility.

Then she plays the trump card. Her eyelashes flutter enticingly, and I feel my resolve shatter.

I nod agreement. And, inwardly, curse myself for being a total sap as I do it.

---

THE BOOKSTORE IS JUST as individualized and distinctive inside as it appeared from the street. I instantly know something is wrong there. Very wrong.

A lot of the time, the feeling is just a tingling in the back of my neck, a nagging sensation like I've forgotten something. Subtle like that. At least, early in the cycle, that is. By the height of the crash, it's like my adrenal glands are running on high speed and I can barely sit still.

Walking into this store, I feel a portion of that rush almost immediately, and it's the most intense feeling of imminent collapse that I've felt from a single business in a long time. I long ago learned to stay away from such places; in my early days in this gig, being in their proximity almost drove me nuts, from the futility of not being able to do anything to help as much as from anything else. I made a pledge to myself to stay away after that, and only frequent businesses that are in good shape.

That's part of the reason I work—worked—at Pete's. He may be a bit of a douche, but he runs a good business.

Two steps into the store, I find I cannot walk further in. My blood is pumping hard, and there's a ringing in my ears that gives strong counterpoint to the bass drum thumping of my heart.

I'm just about to turn and leave when I feel a gentle hand on my arm. I look over to see Gretchen peering intently at me.

"Easy, Tom," she says, and her tone is soothing. But there's a hint of steel beneath.

I give myself a shake and draw a deep breath. Got to get a hold of myself. I'm here. I agreed to be here. Even if the kid's theory is bunk—and it probably is—I committed to trying.

I'm many things, but I don't welch.

I give Gretchen a tight grin, or at least an approximation of one, and nod quickly. "Let's see what we can see."

There's an older woman behind the checkout counter. Plump and grey, with deep smile lines and wearing faux-gold rimmed glasses, the resemblance between her and Charles is obvious. Mom.

Charles leads us over and we exchange introductions all around. Mom—Phyllis—looks taken aback to have not one but two gods in her store. She adjusts the set of her blouse on her shoulders, smooths her jeans, and bobs her head in deep semi-bows to us both.

I have to restrain myself from telling her to stop that.

Over the course of the discussion, it strikes me that she does not seem like a person who is about to lose a long-treasured part of her life. She actually seems at peace with the store's imminent failure. It's not like she's in denial either. She mentions they're going to have a going out of business sale in a couple weeks. But then she jokes about it, saying how she and her husband had been talking about retiring early anyway, and it seems God agrees with that notion.

Which god that would be is another thing I restrain myself from saying.

After a few minutes, another customer comes in and the three of us step over to the periodicals rack.

And watch.

Phyllis is pleasant and efficient in her dealing with the young man. I can find no fault in her customer service. Maybe if she lets us look at the books...

I feel Gretchen's eyes on me and I clear my throat, then try to do something I've not tried in a long, long time. A *long* time. I sit down in a small chair that the store has placed here for reading, close my eyes, and let the feeling of the place wash over me. I don't try to ignore it, don't suppress it. I just...experience.

It's smothering at first. Waves of financial angst flowing over me, into me.

Energizing me.

My heart's beating so hard it actually hurts. My breathing has picked up, and sweat trickles down my brow despite the excellent air conditioning in the place. If I were to stay here for a week, I'd probably leave looking five years younger, the way it's affecting me.

But through it all, I don't get even the vaguest hint of a source, a cause. A reason for the store's issues.

My cynical nature rears back up and snorts inside my head, because what difference does it make? Even if I could sense the root cause at play here, there's nothing I can do about it. I'm a man, not a...

My eyes open as the thought crashes upon my sense of self.

Gretchen is standing in front of me, leaning forward at the waist so she can look directly into my face. She is squinting thoughtfully, her lips pursed. As he eyes meet mine, she nods, ever so slightly.

"Despair," she says, simply. It is a statement of fact, an accurate assessment of my state of mind.

But I jerk back in the chair all the same. It's like she's smacked me. "What?"

Instead of answering, she straightens and turns to regard Charles, who is standing, looking completely awkward with his hands tucked deep into the pockets of his pants, about ten feet away, watching us.

"I think we can do something here," she says, and his brows rise.

I feel mine doing the same. "What?" I say, more forcefully. "No there isn't it. This place is..." I trail off, realizing how loudly I am speaking. I glance back and Phyllis, then look back at Charles. "Look kid, I'm sorry, but there's no saving this place. It's closing no matter what at this point."

He nods. "Oh, I know."

I blink, surprise rendering me speechless.

"I've known for a while now. And as Mom said, we're fine with it. I have other things I want to do, and so do they."

"But -" I manage, but he tramples right over me.

"But then I learned there is such a thing as a god of malinvestment, and I got to wondering. If he exists, why wouldn't he help people like my parents?" He voice is accusing now. "What's wrong with him, if he only just sits back?"

Not *that* pisses me off. I push myself erect and

close him, my jabbing index finger leading the way. "I told you kid, there's nothing I can do. I wish it was different but that's how it is -"

Gretchen's words cut me off and pull the rug out from under my anger at Charles. "Do you really?"

I round on her. "Go screw yourself. You don't know me from -"

"But I do." She closes the distance between us; I hadn't realized she followed me toward Charles as closely as she has. Before I can move away or stop her, she's right up in my face. "We came here to find a problem. It's right here." She taps me on my forehead, between my eyes. "Your despair is just the symptom of a deeper issue. And if you can get past that, you can -"

I'm out the door before she finishes her sentence.

It's the only way to avoid killing them both right then and there.

***

I CANNOT ABIDE BEING PLAYED.

As I storm into my little apartment, the only other thought going through my head is how great it would feel to crush Charles' and Gretchen's windpipes beneath my grasping fingers as I squeeze tighter and tighter and...

I HATE being played.

It's been a long time since I allowed myself to enter a situation where I could even possibly get taken. Why I did it this time is beyond me.

No. No it's not. I know exactly why I fell for it.

But that's not the point. I got played, and I hate getting played.

I hurl my jacket against the wall and have to stop myself from following it up with a glass that I left sitting on the counter. It might be satisfying, shattering the thing, but I will just have to clean it up. And then pay to replace it, and I have very little income right now.

Instead, I heft the glass and pour the last of my scotch into it. I stare at the amber fluid for a long several seconds, and cannot help hearing the last words Gretchen said before I stormed out.

"Just a symptom of a deeper issue."

A little shiver goes through my body as the words strike home. Is it possible?

"Fuck that," I say to myself, then down the scotch in a single swallow.

I need to go get some more.

***

GRETCHEN FINDS me the next morning.

Not exactly a difficult task, considering I came right back to my place from the liquor store and ended up passing out on the floor at the foot of my bed.

When the knock comes on my door, rousing me from a dreamless half-sleep that only served to hasten my hangover, I know immediately who it is.

You may be thinking there's some divine reason for this knowledge. Some psychic link between the deities that lets us know when another is near, like a divine transponder or something. There's not.

Really, it's simple. Who the hell else would be knocking on my door? It's not office hours, and what few friends I have would not ever come by at this time. It sure as hell isn't Charles; after his ploy blew up in his face there's no way he'll be stupid enough to come around my way again.

That just leaves Gretchen. She doesn't strike me as the type to just leave a thing alone once it's stuck in her craw.

I also figure she won't be dissuaded just because I don't answer the door. She'll just hang around, waiting for me to show myself so she can strike. Might as well get it over with.

So I force myself to my feet, down a couple glassfuls of water from the tap in my kitchenette, then hobble over to the door and let her in.

She glances me up and down. "You look like shit." Her tone is crisp, almost clinical, and despite her words there is no judgment in her eyes. They meet mine for a second, then move to look over my shoulder into my place briefly before returning to my face. "Well," she says, and I think maybe her lips turn upward ever so slightly. "Let's go."

I blink, in surprise though I had been sure I would be ready for anything she had to dish out. "Go? Go where?"

Her eyes narrow. "To work."

She turns to her left, toward the elevator at the end of my building's hall, and takes a step away.

"Wait a minute!"

She pauses midway through her next step, turns to look back at me. "Well what are you waiting for?" Then she turns away again.

I watch her depart, not even the faintest desire to go with her intruding on my consciousness. And yet... there is something about her that is, for lack of a better word, compelling.

"God damn it," I snarl, and I grab up my jacket from its little peg near the door.

I catch up with her just as she's pushing the down button.

---

THE PLACE GRETCHEN leads me to is nondescript, a little building near the thinly-defined dividing line between downtown and the suburbs. It once may have been a shop, but now it's boarded up. But, interestingly, it's not abandoned. The place is too kept up for that; no weeds in the lot, and the walkway to the door is clear of trash.

I frown at the building from my position in the passenger seat of her car and shoot a glance at her. I don't trust myself to say anything, though. I'd probably just be nasty, and really she hasn't done anything to deserve that. Yet.

Gretchen catches the look and again I almost think she's about to smile. The impression fades as quickly as it came when she speaks, all business. "What can you tell me about that place?"

I snort. "Seriously?"

Her expression does not waver. She is, apparently, serious.

"I dunno. Abandoned shop of some kind or other. Bums probably live there now."

Gretchen's lips compress slightly and she levels a stare at me so direct that it grabs hold of my eyes and forces them to focus in on hers. I could not look away if I wanted to, and strangely, right this moment I don't feel like I want to. "Anyone can see that," she says. "What *else* can you tell?"

I know what she means. Knew it the first time. But I don't want to go where she's leading. What's the point? I'm about to tell her as much when she lays her hand on my left shoulder. A sort of warmth seems to spread from her touch, and I find myself relaxing. Relaxing completely. And I cannot understand why it seemed so useless to look just a second ago.

So I close my eyes and let myself...just feel.

Almost at once, I can sense it. A pulsing of energy emanating from the little building, subtle, easy to miss, but there nevertheless. Nonetheless, I find myself chagrined for not noticing it before. Normally, I'm fairly well attuned to the flow of commerce around me. I must be really out of it to...

Wait a minute.

I open my eyes and pull free of Gretchen's hand. Immediately, the feeling of relaxation and well-being flees, and I shoot her an accusing look. "What did you do?" I cannot keep the anger from my tone, but she does not flinch away, not even an inch.

"Just a trick I have to help you get over yourself. Nothing monumental." She turns off the car's engine and opens her door. "Coming?"

She moves to get out of the car, but I grab her arm, holding her in place. "What game are you playing at here?"

"I'm trying to help you, Tom." Again her eyes bore into me, and I cannot look away. "Will you let me?"

Ok, that sounds intriguing, I have to admit. So, I shrug and get out of the car.

She leads me to the boarded-up building, then around through the neatly trimmed grass to the building's rear, where a small concrete patio area, about ten feet square, lies in front of a heavy-looking wooden door that looks freshly stained. The doorknob is brass, and a knocker of the same material is mounted in the door's center.

Gretchen lifts the knocker and lets it fall once, and a firm knock rings forth. Almost immediately, the door opens inward a few inches. A dark-haired man with a narrow face and squinty eyes peers at her accusingly.

"You're late."

Gretchen shrugs but says nothing.

The man glances at me and frowns as though he has bitten into a lemon. But after a few seconds, he lets the door swing fully open, then he turns and disappears inside.

We follow him within, and quickly find ourselves descending a narrow staircase into the little building's basement. And there, I receive a big surprise.

Not sure what I expected, but this surely isn't it. The basement is brightly lit and filled with tables for games of all kinds: poker, blackjack, baccarat...I lose track of them all. Along the far wall are a half-dozen slot machines, and a bar is off to the left. To the right, at the immediate bottom of the staircase, is a metal cage that can only be the cashier. Even at this hour of the morning, there are players present. One of the poker tables is full, and two of the blackjack tables. Two ladies are playing the slots, and one middle-aged fellow with receding grey hair and a massive paunch is nursing his sorrows over at the bar.

I know my jaw is hanging open, but I can't help it. "It's a casino," I manage to blurt out, earning an amused look from Gretchen.

"No better place to observe mankind's foibles and tendencies," she says, then adds, "for good or ill."

Not sure if I agree with her assessment, but I figure she's the expert so I let it go.

The man who escorted us turns around and gives Gretchen a direct look. She gives a little shake of her head then turns away from him and veers straight toward the bar. The man meets my eyes and I see, beneath the brusk exterior, a sparkle of something else there. Hopefulness?

Aw, hell.

By the time I reach her side, Gretchen is seated on a bar stool and the bartender has moved away from her toward a collection of bottles at the other end of his domain. Fast work. She turns to put her back to the bar and leans back, resting her elbows on the dark, carved wood of its edge. With nothing better to do, I sit in the stool next to her and turn to follow her gaze toward the gaming tables across the room.

Several seconds pass in silence, and it begins to feel oppressive. I'm pretty sure I know what she wants. The same thing Charles wanted: figure out what's going wrong in the business. By all rights I should just high-tail it, because it won't work any better for her than it did for him. But the simple fact is that moment in the bookstore shook me a bit, and whatever Gretchen did in the car has me intrigued.

And she drove.

So I cross my arms over my chest and wait for her to break the ice.

The bartender returns and sets two glasses of ice water down on the bar near us, then shuffles away. I notice he's giving Gretchen sidelong looks as though he expects her to do something unusual, and I can't help but snorting out a quick chuckle.

She turns to regard me levelly, her nearest eyebrow rising slightly.

I shrug and halfway turn back to the bar so I can pick up my glass. "So what's the plan?" I say, and take a sip.

"You have to ask?"

"Maybe I just want to hear you say it."

The level look becomes chilly for a moment, then, abruptly, she actually lets out a little laugh. "So there *is* more to you than doom and gloom," she says, and retrieves her glass as well. She gives a little nod of her head, but does not drink. "Your predecessor could be quite a charmer. I had hoped it wasn't *all* lost on you."

I choke on the water I'm in the middle of swallowing.

She must know the question I can't ask as I'm regaining my ability to breathe, but instead of answering, she looks back at the games. "Tell me what you see here, Tom." And she lays her right hand on my left.

Immediately I feel that warmth again, spreading from my hand up through the rest of my body, and it's like I've reclined in the most comfortable chair ever. Tension I didn't know I held seems to flee my body and my mind clears completely. I feel calm. Energetic. Focused.

Free.

Without effort, I close my eyes and let my other senses open, and the hum of the place floods through me, palpable in its vibrance. The place is alive with money changing hands, even with so few people here. Mostly from the gamblers to the house, of course, but some the other way. It feels...good.

At first.

After a few seconds, I detect a sour note to the place. And I mean actually sour; I swear I can really taste it, like a lemon. I shudder; I've felt that wrongness before, hundreds—no, thousands—of times, but never so vividly. I let go of my godly sense with a shudder and the foulness leaves my mouth a heartbeat later. Then I open my eyes, and find myself staring at the blackjack table.

At the electronic shuffle machine built into the blackjack table.

Gretchen is looking at me quizzically, her lips pursed slightly. From the corner of my eye, I see her gaze leave me, following my own, and one eyebrow crooks upward. She doesn't speak, but I can see the question on her face.

This has never happened to me before. But I know, beyond a shadow of a doubt. I know.

"The shuffle machine."

Gretchen nods, then takes her hand from mine and stands.

The warmth fades immediately, and all of my cares come crashing back down on me. It's shocking, how heavy that burden is, and I can only watch for a minute as she walks across the room to the man who led us inside. They talk briefly, and his eyes narrow.

What follows is a blur. Two big dudes come into the room through a side door I hadn't noticed before and take up station on either side of the table. Our guide walks over between them and says something quietly, and all play at the table stops.

Hell, all play stops throughout the room.

Gretchen makes a little wave of her hand in my direction to get my attention, then jerks her head toward the stairs before she turns to ascend.

Time to leave, apparently.

---

WE GO to three other businesses. A corner bar in the seedier side of town. A cafe near the waterfront. A gym. All social places of some sort or other; all places where Gretchen apparently knows the owner. After a few minutes in each, and after Gretchen does whatever it is she does, I'm able to focus in and find something wrong. Or at least, I think there's something wrong. We never stay long after I see whatever it is, but hustle out to the next place.

By late afternoon I'm part amused, part bewildered, part excited, and all tired.

She brings me back to my place and I let her in, and there we stand for a moment, just staring at each other. I'm unsure what to say after all of this, and she...

Well, she just has that knowing, serious look on her face, and that makes me even less sure how to break the silence.

Finally, after what seems forever, she gestures toward my little shelf and the new bottle of scotch I got the other day. "Offer a lady a drink?"

I blink, then, with a rueful chuckle, I turn away to pour us both one.

While I'm doing that, her phone rings. She answers quietly, quickly. By the time I turn back around, glasses in each hand, she has hung up and is wearing a little grin that looks almost triumphant.

"You done good, Tom," Gretchen says, accepting her glass with a little nod of her head. "That was Harry, who owns the casino. Guess what they found?"

I shake my head. I have no idea.

"A few of the players somehow rigged the shuffle machine. Seems they had a remote control that set it to shuffle the cards in a pre-determined order, which they had memorized." She raises her glass toward me, offering a toast. "They'd been scamming the place for weeks."

Feeling a bit like someone had just poked me in the chest, hard, I slowly raise my glass as well. She taps hers against mine with a soft CLINK, then takes a drink. I can't see any reason not to, and frankly I rather need a drink right now, so I follow suit.

"I'll wager," she says, "when we hear from the other places we visited today they'll have similar things to say." Her smile grows, and she looks as satisfied as a cat who just found a full milk bowl. "Just like Tisdale."

Again she mentions him. "You knew him?"

"Of course. I've been in this game for a while." She takes another drink. "He was charming, energetic, and driven to help everyone he could. You see, he could tell where they were going wrong. If he caught the problem early enough..." She leaves the rest unsaid. Instead, she just shrugs. "I lost track of him in '25. Only learned he'd passed when I saw you at the meeting in '66." She shakes her head, a frown replacing her earlier triumphant look. "I presumed it was natural causes—a car crash, something like that—and that you..." A sigh escapes her lips. "If I'd known earlier..."

I can only just stare at her for a long several seconds. Finally, tentatively, I manage, "You mean to tell me I've had it all wrong this whole time? That I could have been helping make things better?"

Looking rueful, she nods slowly.

I find that I've slumped down onto the end of my bed, and only long practice keeps me from dropping my scotch to the floor.

Her expression changes, becoming more gentle. "Tom, I can help you. I wasn't sure before today, but I am now."

"What, team up? You do your...whatever it is you do...and I do mine, and together we save businesses everywhere?" I can't stop the sarcastic twitch in my voice as speak, because all the old bitterness is welling up again. And, frankly, I don't know that I like the idea of being her sidekick. Teammate. Whatever.

She surprises me, though. She shakes her head. "That wouldn't work."

Which doesn't make any sense, because didn't it work today?

My expression must speak volumes, because she rolls her eyes slightly. "Oh, it would work, don't get me wrong. But I have other things to do than be your crutch." She leans forward, staring directly into my eyes. "And it wouldn't do *you* any good, not in the long run. No, I can help you get over your," she half-waves toward my head, "issues. In time. With therapy. And when we're done, you'll be able to live up to your potential all on your own." Her eyebrows both rise.

Therapy. Wonderful. Just what I always wanted. I wanted it so bad, I've done my best to stay well clear of it because why do I want some shrink telling me I hate my dad and want to screw my mom, and never mind that she's been dead for decades now. I shake my head. Hard.

Gretchen snorts softly. "It's your choice, of course. But if you don't face down your problems, you'll never get any better, and you'll be left like this," her gesture takes in my crappy little place in all its crapitude, "forever." She pauses, then adds, "Until you decide to be a coward like Tisdale did, and jump off a roof. And then your powers will shift to some other guy with no clue what to do with them, and it'll all start over again."

She downs the last of her scotch and sets the glass down on my little table, then reaches into her purse and pulls out a business card, which she lays on the table next to her glass. "It's up to you, of course."

Then she turns and goes to the door.

I don't try to stop her.

---

I SPEND the next three weeks studiously avoiding that business card.

I get a new job, parking cars for a valet service that contracts with some of the fanciest hotels in town. It doesn't pay so well, but it's enough to cover the bills and I get to meet interesting people and occasionally drive some really sweet cars.

During my off time, I wander the streets, thinking. Feeling the energy of the looming economic crisis as it energizes me. Wondering if what Gretchen said is true, and I really can help instead of just endlessly riding the wave.

I decide to try. I intentionally stop at businesses that are obviously in trouble. I go inside, peruse their wares. *Feel.*

But it never comes together. I can tell there's a problem, but never exactly what it is. Something stops me; I can never get to the calm place that she brought me to, and the answer always eludes me.

Tonight, I'm sitting in my little room nursing the first drink from a new bottle of scotch when a knock on my door interrupts my reverie.

My eyes narrow as I stare at the door, and it takes a minute to realize it's Thursday. Office hours.

Crap.

It's a young couple, mid twenties. They have the look of people who have reached the end of their ropes, but all the same when they greet me there is somehow still some hope in their eyes. A big part of me says I should send them away, not get their hopes up. But what the hell? They already are up.

So I invite them in.

It's the same story I've heard a hundred times before. Their business is on its last leg and they're down to their last pennies, and can I please, somehow help them? Please.

I want to shout at them, tell them I can't help, that it doesn't work that way. But I can't, because I know it's not true.

So I make an appointment with them for tomorrow morning, before I have to be at work. As I let them out, they are smiling. That tiny smidgeon of hope has grown into a bonfire in their eyes, and they practically bounce as they walk, hand-in-hand, down the hallway to the elevator.

I close the door behind them and lean forward, pressing my forehead against the grainy wood. And breathe deeply.

What the hell did I just do?

*It's what you're here for.*

The truth of the thought hits me, and I cannot deny it.

I can help. But not without getting help of my own.

I straighten and walk over to my little table. I set down the glass of whiskey and pick up Gretchen's business card.

Then I pick up my phone.

# MESSAGE FROM THE AUTHOR

Thank you for reading my book. I hope you enjoyed reading it as much as I enjoyed writing it.

Every review helps an author out, so whether you loved this book, hated it, or something in between, please take a minute to tell other readers what you thought. All of the online retailers make it very easy to do, and I would really appreciate it.

Feel free to come say hi at my website or on Facebook. I always enjoy hearing from readers, especially since you all are, collectively, my boss.

I also have a weekly podcast, Story Time With Michael Kingswood, where I read stories and talk through some of the latest goings on in my world. I'd love to see you there.

Thanks again. My best to you and yours.

Warm Regards,
Michael Kingswood

# MAILING LIST

If you enjoyed this book and would like word on new releases and special deals from Michael Kingswood, sign up for his newsletter on his website. Guaranteed to be spam-free, you can opt out at any time. And you can rest assured he will not share your information with anyone, for any reason.

https://michaelkingswood.com/newsletter-signup/

# SUPPORTING PATRONAGE

Michael would like to invite you to become a supporting member of his website. Similar in concept to Patreon, a few dollars a month will give you access to exclusive content, and help him to focus more of his time to writing fun and exciting stories for your enjoyment.

Sign up at his website:

https://www.michaelkingswood.com/membership/
supporting-patronage/

## ABOUT THE AUTHOR

Michael Kingswood is 20-year veteran of the US Navy submarine force and a lifelong fan of science fiction and fantasy literature. His work has appeared in numerous collections and anthologies, to include the Fiction River Anthology series from WMG publishing. He holds a bachelors degree in Mechanical Engineering as well as a Master of Engineering Management and a Master of Business Administration. He has four children and currently resides in San Diego.

Find Michael Kingswood online at:

www.michaelkingswood.com

www.facebook.com/michael.kingswood

steemit.com/@michaelkingswood

# MORE BOOKS BY MICHAEL KINGSWOOD

## Glimmer Vale Chronicles

Glimmer Vale

Out-Dweller

Tollard's Peak

Robbed Blind

Wedding Gifts: A Glimmer Vale Chronicles Story

The Falconer's Stairs

Glimmer Vale Omnibus Edition #1

## The Pericles Conspiracy

Passing In The Night

The Pericles Conspiracy

## Dawn Of Enlightenment

Masters Of The Sun

## Novellas

What Lurks Between

The Necromancer's Lair

The Champion

Veritas Morte

---

## Story Collections

Tales Of Adventure #1

Tales Of Adventure #2

Short Story 10-Pack

A Jar Of Mixed Treats

---

## Short Fiction

Michael has also published a number of shorter works,
links to which can be found on his website.

www.ingramcontent.com/pod-product-compliance
Lightning Source LLC
Chambersburg PA
CBHW032052180726
48284CB00004B/1306